The Creeping Tide

by Gail Herman
illustrated by John Nez

The Kane Press
New York

Acknowledgement: Our thanks to Dr. Jay Hackett, Emeritus Professor of Earth Sciences, University of Northern Colorado for helping us make this book as accurate as possible.

Library of Congress Cataloging-in-Publication Data

Herman, Gail, 1959-
   The creeping tide / by Gail Herman ; illustrated by John Nez.— [1st U.S. ed.].
      p. cm. — (Science solves it!)
Summary: Reluctant to take her little brother to the beach because of his constant questions, a teenager is soon grateful for his newly acquired knowledge of the tides.
   ISBN: 978-1-57565-128-6 (alk. paper)
   [1. Tides—Fiction. 2. Beaches—Fiction. 3. Lost and found possessions—Fiction. 4. Brothers and sisters—Fiction.] I. Nez, John A., ill. II. Title. III. Series.
PZ7.H4315 Cr 2003
[Fic]—dc21

                                                         2002156048

10 9 8 7 6 5 4

First published in the United States of America in 2003 by Kane Press, Inc.
Printed in Hong Kong.
GWP 0610

Science Solves It! is a registered trademark of Kane Press, Inc.

Book Design/Art Direction: Edward Miller

www.kanepress.com

In July I went to day camp. I had outdoor sleepovers with my friend Mark. And I learned to skateboard.

In July my big sister, Kate, got her braces off. (Except she still has to wear a retainer most of the time.)

She looked in the mirror and smiled a lot.

But now it's August.
There is no camp and
Mark is on vacation.
What am I going to do?

"Kate," Mom says one morning. "How about taking Jack to the beach?"

"No way!" says Kate. "He asks too many questions!"

"Can I go?" I ask. "Can we leave right now? Can we stay all day?"

"See, Mom! He's already started," Kate says. "No more questions," I promise. "I won't be any trouble. I'll even make our lunch."

At the beach, there isn't much room to sit. The water covers most of the sand. Finally, I drop our stuff.

I don't ask if Kate likes this spot. That would be a question.

We put on sunscreen. We go for a swim.
Then we lie on the blanket.

I have lots of questions. But I won't say
a thing—at least not to Kate.

I walk over to the lifeguard. Her name is Gwen.
"Have you ever saved anyone's life?" I ask.
"Not yet," Gwen tells me.
"Can you swim across the ocean?" I ask.

"Not yet," she says again.

Let's see. What else can I ask? "What time is it?"

"10:48," Gwen answers.

Then I notice a big sign.

"What's that?" I ask.

"A tide chart," Gwen says. "It tells you when there will be a high tide and when there will be a low tide."

"What's happening now?" I ask.

"The tide is coming in," Gwen says. "The water will keep covering more and more beach until high tide."

Today's Tide
Predictions
(High and Low Waters)

Low	6:03 A.M.
High	11:40 A.M.
Low	5:55 P.M.
High	11:43 P.M.

Gwen helps me read the chart.
High tide is at 11:40 A.M.
"After that, the water will start to move away
from the beach," she tells me.
I check the chart again. Low tide is at 5:55 P.M.
I guess that's when there will be the most beach.

Usually there are 2 high tides and 2 low tides every day.

The water is
farthest up
on the beach
at high tide.

I have another question. "What's the highest tide you ever saw?"

"Once, after a huge storm, the water covered the whole beach—and the parking lot!" Gwen says.

"Wow!" I say.

High 11:40 A.M.
Low   5:55 P.M.
High 11:43 P.M.

GWEN

Then I ask, "What do you like better, high tide or low tide?"

"I like to dig for clams and look for sea animals, so low tide is my favorite," Gwen says.

I am about to ask, "Can I go clam-digging with you?" But Gwen looks kind of tired.

Then I hear Kate calling, "Lunch time!"

Today's Tide
Predictions
(High and Low Waters)

Low	6:03 A.M.
High	11:40 A.M.
Low	5:55 P.M.
High	11:43 P.M.

GWEN

I race to our blanket and take out the food.
"Yum! Peanut butter sandwiches!" says Kate.
"I couldn't eat them when I still had braces."
She takes out her retainer, and we both eat.

Then Kate says, "A cold mango smoothie would taste good right now. Let's go to the snack stand."

It's pretty far away, but I don't mind.
There's lots to see.

We stop to watch a sand castle contest.
One man slips and sits on his own castle.

"Oops!" I say.

We stop to watch the sailboats. After a
while we stop again to watch a girl fly a kite.
The kite looks like a monster—kind of like
Kate when she's in a bad mood.

We finally get to the snack stand. Kate sees some friends and they talk and talk. I wait so long I get thirsty again.

SNACK SHACK

Kate buys me another smoothie and we walk back—past the sailboats and the sandcastles and the girl flying a kite.

When we get back to our spot, the blanket is sandy and wet.

"Hey!" says Kate. "The sunscreen is missing. And your goggles. And my retainer! Somebody stole it!"

"Why would someone take your retainer?" I almost ask. But no questions.

Instead, I think. I think about the sand castles. How on the way back there was more sand for building.

And how the girl with the kite was standing on sand—not in the water.

The water is moving away from the beach!

Gwen walks past. "What time is it?" I ask her.

"Almost five o'clock," she tells me.

"How can you ask such a silly question when our stuff is missing!" Kate says.

But it's not silly. I'm trying to figure out what happened.

I walk in a straight line, and step over seaweed that has washed onto shore. The sand is wet and wavy.

There are tide pools in the sand. I stare into the big puddles the ocean has left behind.

Seashells! Crabs! Little fish!

They are all here! I stoop closer.

You can find creatures like starfish and sea urchins in tide pools, too.

"Jack!" my sister calls. "What are you doing?"
Oh, that's right. Her retainer.

The tide washes all kinds of things onto the beach—driftwood, feathers, shells . . . Some of these things come from thousands of miles away.

I walk almost to the water. "Aha!" I spot the sunscreen. And my goggles.

Just as I thought. High tide came in while we were gone.

The waves washed over our blanket and carried our things down the beach.

But still . . . no retainer.

I turn around to go back and—ouch! I step on something a little sharp. The retainer!

Kate runs over. "How did you find it?" she asks.

"I just followed the tide," I tell her.

She gives me a big hug.

"Go ahead," she says. "You can ask me one question."

I look at her and smile. "Can we come back tomorrow?"

THINK LIKE A SCIENTIST

Jack thinks like a scientist—and so can you!

Scientists infer. They use what they see or observe to help explain why or how something happens. You infer, too. You see someone open an umbrella. So you infer that it's raining.

Look Back

On pages 12-13 Jack observes that the water is covering most of the sand. What does he infer from his observation? Compare pages 18-19 with page 21. What do you observe? What can you infer?

Try This!

What can you infer about the tide from looking at each picture?

A.

B.

C.

Answers:
A. The tide is going out.
B. The tide is coming in.
C. It is low tide.

32